BROKEN FEATHER

VERLA KAY

ILLUSTRATED BY STEPHEN ALCORN

G. P. PUTNAM'S SONS • NEW YORK

Broken Feather,
Native boy.
Filled with spirit,
Strength and joy.

Bows and arrows,
Corn-husk pouch.
Bushes rustle,
Natives crouch.

Small voice, whisper,
"Father, who?"
"White men hunting,
Passing through."

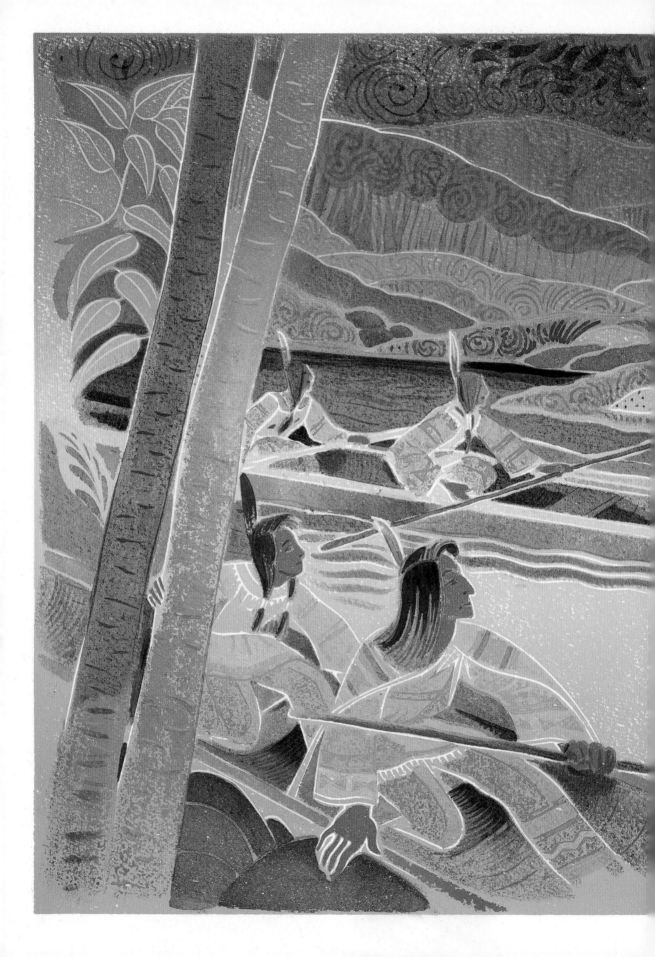

Gunshots echo,
Hunters ride.
Natives silent,
Dugouts glide.

River rushing,
Churning, brown.
Laced with eddies,
Swirling down.

Stabbing, spearing,
Salmon, trout.
Broken Feather,
Joyous shout.

Rocks and dead wood,
Dry leaves, bark.
Puffing, blowing,
Tiny spark.

Red flame flickers,
Warming hands.
Sunset glowing,
Painting lands.

Wise men chanting,
Tall, proud stance.
Natives singing,
Feathered dance.

Charcoal darkness,
Crescent moon.
Night wind whispers,
Masked raccoon.

Gold sun rising,
Horned lark sings.
Eagle soaring,
Spreading wings.

Bushes rustle,
Horses snort.
White men riding,
Far from fort.

Broken Feather,
"They're so near."
Father frowning.
"Moving here.

"Bringing wagons,
Cutting trees,
Building houses
Where they please."

Warriors chanting,
Big drums, beat.
Angry faces,
Stomping feet.

Fight for homeland,
Hide, retreat.
Valiant battles,
Sad defeat.

War-torn nation,
Fighting done.
Silent rifles,
Setting sun.

Broken Feather,
Sleep mat rolled.
Woods deserted,
Fire pit, cold.

Empty lodges,
Forced to tramp.
Natives marching,
Brown eyes, damp.

Reservation,
Anguished cry.
Broken Feather,
"Father, why?"

"They were many,
We were few.
Now, my son,
It's up to you."

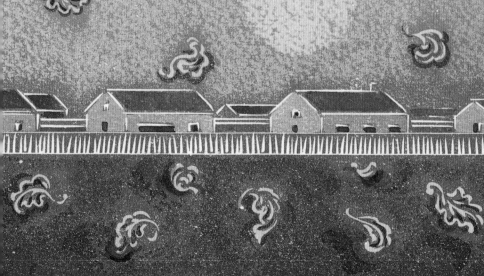

Native warriors,
Chanting loud.
Broken Feather,
Standing proud.

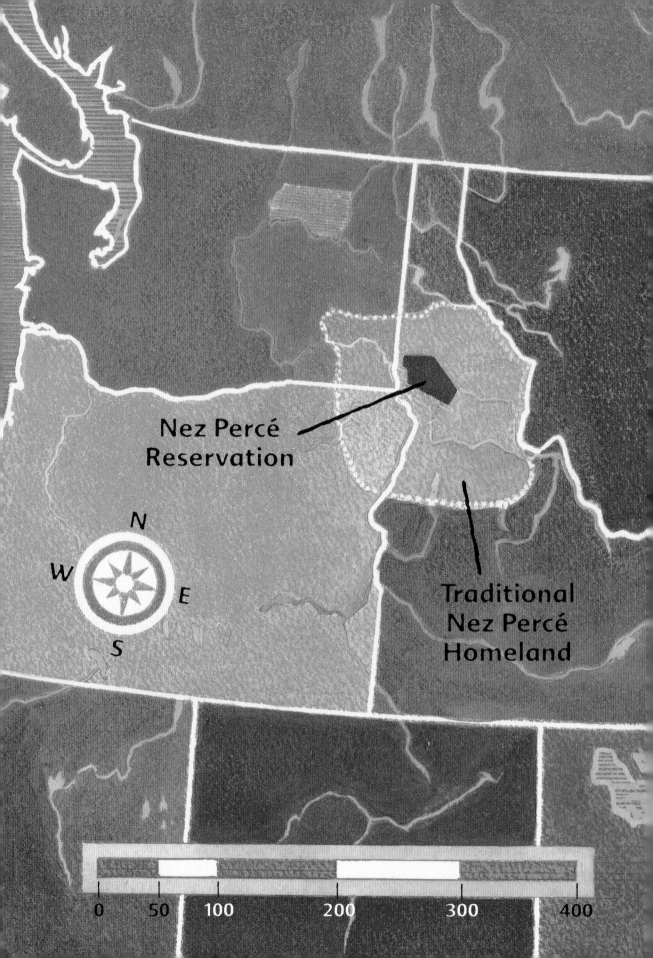

Nez Percé
Reservation

Traditional
Nez Percé
Homeland

N
W   E
S

0   50   100   200   300   400

AUTHOR'S NOTE: Broken Feather was not real, but his story was. His story is also the story of many Native Americans of his time. A trip to the Nez Percé reservation and their museum in Idaho inspired me to incorporate some of their historical facts into Broken Feather's story. It wasn't possible for me to include every detail of this tribe's fascinating history and way of life, so I focused on one thing—the fact that the Nez Percé were a gentle people, driven to war when their homelands were forcibly taken from them. They traveled seasonally over a large area of the American West. They lived in tepees during their summer travels and in lodges in permanent villages the rest of the year. After the Nez Percé War in 1877, they were placed on a reservation in what is now the state of Idaho.

It is my fervent hope that this story will allow today's children to experience some of the joy and pride the Nez Percé people have in their heritage, and that it will help them understand a little of what it meant to be a Native American at a time when Europeans were relentlessly expanding into their homelands.

—Verla Kay

ILLUSTRATOR'S NOTE: As a maker of relief-block prints, one of the challenges I relish most lies in finding ways in which to bring the barren, uncut surface of a block to life. While the creative process may be unforgiving (to begin with, what one cuts away cannot be put back!), the inherent constraints of this particular medium may also serve to force the dedicated printmaker to be wonderfully inventive, daring, and resourceful. As poet Richard Wilbur remarked, noting that the limitations imposed by poetic form can produce powerful imagery, "The strength of the genie comes of his/her being confined in a bottle." To this phenomenon I trace the source of my long-standing fascination with this age-old medium.

The imagery I have created for this volume is imbued with a delicacy of line, color, and tonal gradation that owes as much to the nuance of watercolor and oil painting as to the stark severity of traditional relief-block printmaking. Broken Feather, the tender protagonist of this book, saw his world unfold through the impressionable eyes of youthful innocence. Now I, by filtering my visions of his fading world through spectrums of lush, sensuous color (reminiscent of a rainbow), seek to pay homage to the purity of his spirit.

—Stephen Alcorn

With heartfelt thanks to
Josiah Pinkham and the Nez Percé tribe
for all their assistance
with my research of this book.

To my dear friends
Pam Ledwick and Jana Evans
for believing in me, and to
Michele Tennant and Bonnie Hernandez
for their invaluable critique help.

—V. K.

For Professoressa Roberta Mugnai
Sezione di Arti Grafiche
Istituto Statale d'Arte, Florence, Italy

Con gratitudine e profonda ammirazione.

—S. A.

Text copyright © 2002 by Verla Kay. Illustrations copyright © 2002 by Stephen Alcorn. All rights reserved. This book, or parts thereof, may not be reproduced in any form without permission in writing from the publisher, G. P. Putnam's Sons, a division of Penguin Putnam Books for Young Readers, 345 Hudson Street, New York, NY 10014. G. P. Putnam's Sons, Reg. U.S. Pat. & Tm. Off. Published simultaneously in Canada. Printed in Hong Kong by South China Printing Co. (1988) Ltd. Designed by Gina DiMassi. Text set in Advert Rough. The illustrations in this book, polychrome relief-block prints, were printed by hand, using oil-based inks on Saunders Waterford watercolor paper (140 lb., cold pressed). The finishing touches were provided via the application of subtle oil glazes. Library of Congress Cataloging-in-Publication Data   Kay, Verla. Broken Feather / Verla Kay; illustrated by Stephen Alcorn.   p. cm.   1. Indians of North America—Juvenile poetry. 2. Children's poetry, American. [1. Indians of North America—Juvenile poetry. 2. American poetry.] I. Alcorn, Stephen, ill. II. Title. E99+ 811'.54   00-041504 ISBN 0-399-23550-7
1 3 5 7 9 10 8 6 4 2
First Impression